GBAELAY

GOES DOWN MEMORY LANE

By: Dr. Jasoe

THE
FAMILIAR
UNKNOWN

To my kids, nieces, nephews,
and little cousins; never be afraid
to make your dream a reality

Table of Contents

BROKEN DREAM

It was the first day of school, and Mamma dropped me off early like she always did since I started school. Because she had to be at

1

work early, I got dropped off before most kids. Our principal let us, the early kids, hang out in the school lobby.

"She has no idea how much of a help she is," Mamma would say before letting me out of the car, but not without my 'see you later'

kiss. Mamma would wait until I ran into the building before driving off.

This morning, as soon as I entered, I saw Mr. Langley standing right at the door greeting the kids.

"Good morning, Gbaelay," he said.

"Wow, you know my name and even said it right?" I said so softly. I don't think he heard me because he had already begun asking me a question.

"Are you glad to be back, Gbaelay?"

"Yes, sir!" I uttered excitedly. "Summer this

year was great as always," I continued, "but I missed my friends at school."

Mr. Langley was the school counselor. He never got out of his office much. He knew my name and even said it right! That was the first sign that I would have a great school year.

After I told him a little about my summer and how I was happy to be back to school, he told me he didn't have much of a summer. I thought that was weird. I knew he never left his office, but I had no idea that he was stuck in that office even during the summer months.

"It was all about getting things done. The story of my life," He added as he scratched his head.

Now I was more confused, but I smiled and let him think I understood what he had just said.

"Who is your teacher this year, Gbaelay?"

"Ms. Boatwright," I said with the largest grin on my face.

"Ms. Boatwright is not coming back this year, but don't worry, you have a fantastic teacher taking over."

"Please don't say, Ms. Rain, please don't say Ms. Rain," I mumbled those words, at the same time saying a secret prayer. Then, just like that, it came out, "Ms. Rain will be teaching grade two this year. She is taking over Ms. Boatwright's class." He revealed. "Isn't that so kind of her?"

I was hoping that was one of those questions that people ask, but don't really expect an answer. Either way, I had way bigger issues on my mind than Ms. Rain's sacrifice.

At that very moment, I felt a hot drop of a tear on my one cheek. It must have been invisible because Mr. Langley laughed and stated, "Fantastic teacher equals fantastic school year!"

All the teachers, for some reason, thought Ms. Rain was a 'fantastic' teacher. That was something we kids did not bother finding out for ourselves. All I knew at this moment was that, for the first time in my life, I hated school and I wanted to reset my summer vacation.

I think I was more sad and scared than worried.

Either way, I wanted the summer vacation to reset and go back to when school first ended in May.

Every student in my school knew Ms. Rain was mean!

The children in her class were always quiet in the hallway. During assembly, they sat down and looked straight ahead and won't dare twitch or fidget.

I heard from some of the big kids that they didn't think she liked kids. They said that she would make a kid cry just by looking at them. She had the 'Rain Look.'

I was told that one day, during assembly, a boy in her class thought he heard someone call his name and turned around. She gave him the 'Rain Look.' The next two days, afraid of what would become of him, the boy stayed home.

I tried to hide my fear, but Mr. Langley noticed anyway.

"You had such a great year in the first grade and I know you will have a great school year this year," encouraged Mr. Langley.

I managed to quickly put on a smile. Except, it was that smile I use with Mamma's friends at church.

"Well I don't know about that," I said to myself as I scurried away to the morning waiting area. Maybe it was because it was a new school year or something, but the bell took forever to ring, leaving me to replay what I had just heard.

The busy morning hallway traffic was continuing without a pause, but I had no time to pay attention to anything. I heard a few hellos and other happy-return-to-school-ness, but nothing could distract me from what was going on in my head. I was focused on coming up with a plan. I needed a great plan on how I would explain to Mamma that I wanted to transfer to another school.

I don't remember anyone else sitting next to me or trying to talk directly to me. My mind was too busy making plans for my new school.

FACING MY FEAR

"Cliiiing, cling, cling, cling, clinnnng," went the sound of the bell coming from the principal's office. The never-ending, loud, obnoxious sound

23

of the bell took me out of my daze. That's when I noticed that everyone had left for their classrooms. I slowly got up and grabbed my backpack that I had laid in front of me, unattended.

As heavy as my body felt, I still managed to walk toward my classroom.

I stood by the classroom door, hoping other kids were already in there.

The silence from the room told me that there were no other students in the classroom. Other than the usual sounds of a teacher's 'busyness,' there was nothing — not one student.

I think they'd all found out about Ms. Rain and decided not to come back to this school.

'Poor me, why didn't I find out earlier like everyone else?' Sadness took over my thoughts, removing fear for a brief moment. For some reason, that felt more comforting – but only for a brief moment.

I had no choice in that moment but to comfort myself. I told myself it would be okay, but my heart wouldn't listen. It was beating so fast and loud, that anyone standing next to me would have heard it.

I started to feel sick. My stomach felt stirred up, sort of like I wanted to both barf and do a number two at the same time.

"Great!" I said to myself.

Now I had a reason to go home- a real reason to go to the office and call Mamma. She said that I should call her if I felt sick.

'OH NO, now my head is aching?' The pounding of my head matched that of my heart. I opened and shut my eyes a few times, but that didn't seem to help anything.

'This is better than perfect; I really am sick. The timing is perfect. When I call Mamma, after hearing all of my symptoms, she won't even think to tell me to try and finish the day.'

Stomach ache, headache, and heart problems are a big deal! They are the kind of things that will even put you in the hospital. I hate hospitals but at this moment, I would settle for whatever I could get, as long as it would buy me time to figure out how I could avoid being in Ms. Rain's class.

In fact, I thought I would not be back at school for a while. Maybe a long while, even.

"Come on in; you can wait for the others in here as you unpack," Ms. Rain yelled, terrifying me even more.

'That was not the plan, that was NOT the plan, THAT WAS NOT THE PLAN!' I repeated about a million times to myself.

Suddenly, my body started to move toward the door without me even doing anything. I was at the classroom door within seconds.

Even with my quiet creep toward the door, Ms. Rain heard me. "Hello there, what's your name?" She asked. "Gbaelay. My name is Gbaelay, ma'am."

"Bailay, nice to meet you. I'm Ms. Rain, your teacher this year."

"Hello Ms. Rain," I said softly, almost as though I didn't want to be heard.

She asked me how my summer vacation was. I managed to say it was fun. I tried to walk away so she won't say anything mean to me.

Suddenly, she said, "That's nice, Bailay." She said my name wrong again, but I wasn't about to correct her. I couldn't imagine how much worse my life would be if I did.

"Did you do anything special this summer?" She continued while fumbling with her papers.

"Wow! She's still being nice," I thought to myself, "doesn't she hate kids?" Maybe she was being nice because she heard the pounding of my heart and the roaring of my stomach. I briefly smiled because her knowledge of my sickness was a plus for me.

Anyhow, I decided to play along and, magically, the rhythm of my heart and head were moving at a slower pace. That's when I noticed that my body was not as tensed

anymore; it had relaxed a little.

I told her I was away for most of the summer.

"Where did you go?" She asked.

"To Baltimore. I have family there." I went on to tell her how it was and that I visited there every summer. "Mamma lets me spend the summer with my cousins in Baltimore."

"Wow," Said Ms. Rain, "I went to Baltimore too. It was fun, but I was only there for the July fourth weekend. Did you get to see any firework shows?" she continued.

"I DID!" I said, and I immediately felt everything in me light up. I went to the Inner Harbor.

I think it was in that very moment I forgot that I was terrified of Ms. Rain. I started talking on and on. Before you knew it, I was offering to show her my pictures from Baltimore.

"That's a great idea, Bailay. We have our introductory show-and-tell coming up next week, and you can bring your pictures to share with the class. I'll wait for everyone to come in and make the announcement."

"I'm glad someone is as excited to be back to school as much as I am," she said with a smile. Just like Mamma, she was already reading my mind.

"She's excited to come back to school? Really? I thought she hated kids. Wow, I like Ms. Rain already!" I whispered to myself. And, just like that, I realised my sickness had disappeared.

THRILLED

When I got home, I couldn't stop myself from talking. I went on and on, explaining my day to Mamma. She said that I was saying one thousand words per second. That's what Mamma says when she wants to say that I am talking faster than regular people.

"Mamma," I said softly, "can you help me find some of my pictures from all the times I visited Baltimore?"

"Sure, GeeGee, remind me when I call you on my way home from work tomorrow."

"OK, Mamma."

Mamma has this thing where she always wants to be in the right 'mental mode' to do things. I don't understand why, but what I do know is that when she is in her mental mode, things get done - and in a fun way.

When tomorrow came, I did as Mamma had instructed me. I called her and that made her ready to start the moment she walked through the door. Mamma quickly changed and, within minutes, we were opening the doors to the shed.

The shed in the back of our house is like a magical vault. It has everything. I mean, E-VER-RY-THING. Mamma says the things are all important and memorable, but I think memorable is just the word grown-ups use to mean old-people-stuff they are attached to.

Boxes and plastic bins are stacked up in piles. There are clothes that Mamma said will fit her again someday and CDs, cassettes, and records with songs you could just listen to on YouTube or download on iTunes.

Most of all were boxes with books that had pictures. Some looked like scrapbooks, others Mamma said were albums, and some were just in these packets that looked like envelopes, except they were wider and bigger. There were pictures on these strips that looked like plastic and were see-through. When you looked at it very closely, you could see a tiny version of the actual pictures on them. Mamma called them films.

The pictures must have been packed in some kind of order because Mamma knew exactly where to look for what.

She started taking out pictures and telling stories that the pictures reminded her of.

"Oh, how I miss my college days! This was when I was at the peak of my cool game." She uttered. I was trying to hold back my chuckle but, then, she put her hands on her waist and rolled her neck as she snapped her fingers. Without warning, my chuckle came out, turning into an uncontrollable laugh.

"MAMMA," I yelled hysterically, "you know you

can't do that in public, right? No, actually, please do not ever do that in public. Never, Mamma, please promise!" Then we both laughed for about a whole minute, or even longer.

I love Mamma, but I

had to tell her that old people 'coolness' was supposed to be kept secret. She did her snapping and rolling neck thing again. I covered my eyes. We both laughed, and then continued rummaging through the photos.

THE DRIFT AWAY

The next box Mamma picked up made her give a long, sorrowful sigh and pause for what felt like millions of minutes. She quietly started going through the pictures. As she did, she had this sad look on her face; then, her eyes grew big, followed by a smile.

Mamma always got that look whenever she talked about 'home.' Home is

Liberia, where Mamma and her parents were born. She was always talking about all the great memories she had while growing up in Liberia.

I stretched out my arms to grab some of the pictures Mamma was looking at and, suddenly, she went into this state. She was still in the shed physically, but everything else was gone.

"Mamma? Mamma?" I called out twice and then she was 'back.' "Sorry, GeeGee, did you say something?" She stated, "I must have slipped down memory lane." Whenever she talked about memory lane, in my mind I saw this invisible place where people could disappear to without moving a muscle.

"Mamma, can you take me with you to memory lane

one day?" "Well, you will go there one day, GeeGee, you will," She promised.

As she spoke, Mamma started pulling pictures from her first visit back to Liberia after she and her parents left. This was long before I was born; even long before she met Daddy.

"Liberia is along the coast, so it has many beautiful beaches."

"This picture was taken on Tropicana Beach, close to where I grew up." She mentioned, "One of my childhood best friends had a party and invited me."

"This is Lake Piso," She continued, showing me another beautiful picture. "I remember how relaxing it felt just being at this place."

"These are pictures of different beaches in Buchanan, which I used as my hideout when I wanted to get away from the bustling city life."

"Gosh, these pictures are beautiful," I babbled to myself.

I don't think I had seen any undeveloped beaches as beautiful as the ones in Mamma's pictures.

"Yes, GeeGee, all of these are beautiful, but my favorite of all is visiting my parent's town."

She pulled out pictures of the place she referred to as Todee. There was nothing special about this place, but she went on and on about how kind everyone was.

"Once they heard we were visiting, they wanted

to come and pay their respects. My dad and I always went together, which made me feel really important because people loved him."

Mamma then showed me a picture of her and at least five other people in a huddle, eating together out of the same bowl.

"Everyone had a story to tell." She added, "We sat down eating and talking about the good old days. I honestly did not remember any of the stories, but the fun made me pretend I remembered so they could keep telling them."

Mamma went on and on about how, after their meal, she would walk around inhaling the freshness of the town and taking pictures with people and of everything in sight.

"That explains some of these mysterious and random pictures," I said to myself.

THE DISCOVERY

I was starting to get tired, but didn't want to hurt Mamma's feelings because she sure was enjoying telling her stories.

75

Not that I didn't like hearing them, but I was starting to think maybe we should leave some for next time. As I was still pretending to be listening, I was digging through the pictures and, bam! I pulled out the cutest, silkiest brown-ish and cream strap scarf. "Look, Mamma," I said excitedly. "Oh my goodness, is this where that has been?" She uttered.

"This is a scarf I got from your great grandma before moving to America. I thought it was missing."

That led to another 30 minutes of stories about this great grandma.

"Are you guys going to need more time?" The voice startled us. That was Daddy. "DADDY!" I screamed. I stretched out my arms and drew my hands

back toward me, touching
the middle of my chest. I
did that twice. That's
Daddy and I's 'pretend hug.'
I was buried in Mamma's
memories so, of course, I
couldn't get my usual real
hug.

Daddy found a spot on the floor and somehow, with him being there, Mamma told fewer stories and the ones she told were even shorter. Within a short time, we were done and cleaning up for dinner.

THE ANTICIPATION

We must have been really hungry and tired, because dinner was fast and quiet. As soon as we

81

cleaned up, it was my bedtime.

I made sure the pictures for my show and tell were tucked away in my backpack. I was ready for everyone to hear my story about my trip.

Once I was done, Daddy

came in and gave me my usual goodnight kiss - which usually turned into one of those daddy-daughter pep talks, a few 'I love you's, some 'I'm always here for you's, and a whole bunch of other mushy talk.

But, before he could

finish, I was 'drooling', as Daddy would say.

THE BIG DAY

On the presentation day, I sat in my seat listening to everyone tell their story and showing whatever piece or artifact they had. Everyone's story sounded like an adventure. They made me want to be there. Even Mary-Rose had everyone clapping when she was done - she talked about her family in Kenya. She had a PowerPoint of all the pictures and even actual things she brought back were passed out to the class.

Mary-Rose has always been that one student you could count on to do less work than you in class. She has always been my best friend, but I never understood how she never got excited about learning.

Seeing how much effort Mary-Rose had put into her work worried me. Not because I wasn't happy for her, but because I felt like she had more information about Ms. Rain and did not want to be "that student."

If Mary-Rose was going

above and beyond to avoid being on Ms. Rain's bad side, then I had no choice but to go above and beyond.

What was I going to do now? I didn't want Ms. Rain to not like me; that would be very bad. 'A trip to Baltimore? What's so special about that?' I thought to myself. That's when it hit me - I was so close to being liked by Ms. Rain. 'OH, BOY!'

Deep in my thoughts again, I barely heard Ms. Rain call on me.

"Yes, Ms. Rain," I said softly.

"We might not have that much time for your

presentation, would you mind waiting till tomorrow?"

'Wait, did I hear that correctly? Did she say tomorrow?'

"Yes, Ms. Rain, no problem. Tomorrow will be great." I had to repeat it to make sure I heard her right, just hoping she didn't change what I thought she had said.

We cleaned up and were ready to go home.

THE CHANGE OF PLANS

All I did when I got home was think about how to make my presentation better than Mary-Rose's. I rewrote and rewrote and rewrote, but that did nothing. I even practiced my presentation over and over again. It was a boring presentation to make, so that's how I knew it would be boring for people to listen to.

Mamma said to take a break and have a snack, as maybe it would come to me. I agreed only because I wanted the snack, but I had no hope that anything was going to come to me.

I opened the fridge and saw some Kahyan – a

Liberian snack made from dried grated cassava, roasted peanuts, and sugar blended together. The light bulb in my head came on as bright as it could! That kahyan was my clue to the best presentation.

"MAMMA, MAMMA!" I

screamed, feeling the effect in my throat. "MAMMA, I GOT IT! I GOT IT, MAMMA!" I continued.

I completely ignored what she was saying and excitedly started to tell her I was going to change my idea for my presentation.

"Isn't it a little too late for that, GeeGee?" She voiced as she softly rubbed my hair.

"Momma, okay, so listen," I said. I told her that I wanted to do my presentation on her visit to Liberia. "I will use the scarf as my artifact and speak a little about your side of the family!"

"I'm listening," she interrupted, making that face that makes one of her eyebrows go up.

Then I started the presentation. I didn't realize how much I had remembered. I started to do that one-thousand-words-per-second talking that Momma talks about.

When I was done, even Momma was impressed - but

not in that I'm-doing-it-

because-you-are-my-child

way, she was really

impressed!

"I can't wait to hear

what everyone thinks about

your presentation.

So proud of you,

GeeGee." She kissed me on

the top of my head as I packed up my backpack for school.

DOWN MEMORY LANE

I entered the school,

skipping with excitement. I

was so ready for my

presentation and nothing was going to change that. I was sure my presentation would make Ms. Rain realize I was her favorite student ever.

When we got to class, Ms. Rain made her morning announcement, did her mini-lesson, and we completed our classwork. Then, it was time for my presentation.

I would normally be nervous, but not today. I stood in front of the class with the biggest grin.

"We're ready whenever

you are, Bailay" Ms. Rain stated.

"Good morning everyone, my name is Gbaelay, and I just got back from the West African country of Liberia."

I wanted to make my presentation as real as

possible, so I pretended I had just returned from a trip to Liberia. I could see the expression on everyone's face. They liked my introduction and that was my clue to keep going. I wanted the class to feel what I felt when I listened to Mamma's story.

Instead, I got really

consumed by the story and

couldn't figure out what was

happening to me. I even

added some extra details

about my great grandma.

Then, suddenly, I felt

like the way you would feel

when sleeping. Almost like

you are watching yourself, but you can't control what you were doing. I felt like I was in the classroom, but not really there. I think I just went down memory lane. It felt magical.

Mamma was right, it was just a matter of time.

When I was done with my presentation, I took the scarf out of the bag, opened it up, and started explaining what Mamma had told me about the scarf. Then, I told the class all about the scarf and how long Mamma has had it and how she had passed it on to me. I decided to pass it around the class so that everyone could touch it and know what it felt like.

Mary-Rose was the closest student to me, so, I passed it to her first. "WOW!" she uttered uncontrollably.

As the scarf went around the room, kids started to raise their hands. They all wanted to ask questions. Most of the questions were about Africa. I didn't have real detailed answers to the questions they were asking, but I think I did my best.

When the scarf was back in my hands, I tied it on my head and took a bow, and the class started clapping. They clapped so hard that it made my smile big and wide. I even got a high five from Ms. Rain. I don't think she could hide her appreciation for my presentation, even if she tried.

There is no way Ms. Rain was going to have even the littlest dislike for me.

That very moment, for the first time in my life, I didn't mind being the teacher's pet. In fact, the thought of it made me smile big and wide again.

I drifted into my thoughts again but could still hear the clapping. 'Yes,' I said to myself, 'this is indeed going to be the best school year ever.'